PREACHER MAN

Volume 2
The Devil & All His Works

Murray Pura

First Edition

Published by
Helping Hands Press

ISBN: 978-1-62208-515-6

Printed in the United States of America

PROLOGUE

"We are ready to worship, Herr Kroeger."

The tall and narrow man in a black SS officer's uniform looked up from his desk, a cup of tea in one hand. "So soon?"

His young aide, also in a black SS uniform, nodded. "We were able to abduct a woman sooner than expected. She was on her own in the backcountry. It will appear to authorities as if she missed her step and tumbled over a precipice into a chasm. The chasm is impossibly deep. They will not send anyone in to retrieve a body."

"And you have rendered her compliant?"

"Yes."

"*Gut.*" The older man rose, glancing down at his desk and then at the portraits of Hitler and Jesus on the wall across from him. "I was reading about the new wing of our White Christ movement in America; it is just getting on its feet. In Montana. They will be trying out some different ideas, using some new incantations to see how large of a populace they can bring under their control in as short a time as possible. If they are successful with their experiments we may make use of some of their discoveries here in Europe."

"*Jawohl, mein Kommandant.*"

"Skeritt is heading it up. He was here last summer."

1

"I remember, sir. Perfect blonde hair, perfect blue eyes, the perfect Aryan."

"Indeed. I look forward to receiving his reports. We must bring up Skeritt and his coven in our worship today." He moved out from behind his desk. "Do you have my robe ready?"

"Yes, sir, it is in your private washroom."

"The goat's head is up? The pentagram in place?"

"Everything is in order for the ritual."

"Who is wielding the knife?"

"Herr Himmler."

"Ah, yes, Himmler, a most fortunate family name and bloodline. He's very good at this sort of thing, isn't he? Making the cuts, getting as much blood as possible?"

"He is, Herr Kroeger."

They left the room, the young man trailing the older man.

"Today is the Spring Equinox," Kroeger said. "It is essential to nourish it with fresh blood. The problem is finding virgins in this godless and promiscuous age. Was this established after the abduction?"

"Yes, sir. She is entirely suitable for sacrifice to our lord."

The older man smiled. "What a blessing."

1

City of Diamondback
Anaconda County
Montana
August 2014

Pastor Jude Aaron Blackstone brought his Jeep Rubicon to a sudden stop. A deputy sheriff in a khaki uniform had blocked the street with his patrol car and was holding up his hand.

Blackstone powered down his window. "What's up, deputy?"

"A parade is going by here in five, sir."

"A parade? The rodeo's not in town for weeks."

"This doesn't have anything to do with the rodeo."

"What is it then?" demanded Blackstone.

"A church group."

"A church group?" Blackstone thought over what other pastors in the community had told him about their summer plans. "Which one?"

The deputy shrugged. "Beats me." He walked past the jeep towards vehicles lining up behind Blackstone. "There will be about a ten minute delay," Blackstone heard him announce to the other drivers. "We have a parade on its way."

Blackstone turned off the jeep's engine and waited. In a couple of minutes, he heard loud shouting and saw flags and banners coming from his left. Several of the flags were red and white and black, but he could not make out the symbols on them. The marchers wore black T-shirts and tiger stripe camo pants and black military boots. There were crests on their shirts composed of red swastikas and white death's heads. Men and women had clean-shaven heads. At the same time as he was taking all this in, the symbols on the flags became obvious to Blackstone – blood red swastikas on fields of black with white death's heads around which rattlesnakes were coiled, fangs bared, ready to strike. The shouts also became clear – *White Power! White Nation! Sieg Heil!*

Blackstone looked out his window at the deputy who was standing by the side of his patrol car. "Are you kidding me?"

"Free country," replied the deputy, keeping his eye on the marchers.

"Not if they get control of it."

There were about one hundred of them. Some mothers were pushing babies in strollers as they chanted. Most kept thrusting their fists into the air as they yelled the same phrases over and over again. Several helped hold long black banners covered in red swastikas and white skulls and large crimson letters that spelled out MONTANA JUSTICE MOVEMENT. Underneath the red letters was another one of the coiled rattlesnakes, jaws gaping. Another flag was entirely white, but for a black symbol of Odin's Cross – he knew Odin was the supreme god, the Allfather of the gods in Norse and German mythology, and the ruler of Asgard, one of the Nine Worlds, along with his wife. Blackstone felt two things go through him – a gut revulsion to the swastikas and Odin's Cross and the cries of white power. And the sharp cut of something deeper and darker that hit like a bullet and made him bleed inside.

"*Zabolus,*" he whispered.

A few minutes after they had passed the deputy got into his patrol car and sped away. Blackstone drove a few blocks north and a few blocks east and parked at the Sheriff's Office.

"Oh, Pastor Jude." A young woman with short blond hair and a deeply tanned face looked up from her computer. "Sheriff Youngblood won't be in for another half hour at least."

"We had an appointment, Sierra."

"He knows. " Her smile was big.

"Did he forget about the march?"

"There was an incident."

"What sort of incident?"

"The congregation of Beth Shalom were assembled by the 7-11 on the march route. They were protesting."

"Can't they do that?"

"There was a scuffle."

"A scuffle?" Blackstone headed back out the door. "I'd better check on that."

Sierra got to her feet. "Please don't, Jude. I mean, Pastor Jude."

"Why not? You afraid I'll make things worse?"

"Yes."

"Is this about the man I shot six months ago?"

"The sheriff advised me you might want to intervene if you heard about Beth Shalom clashing with the Montana Justice Movement. He asked me to request that you stay here and wait for him."

"He figured that if you asked me that would be enough?"

"For a gentleman like you, yes."

Blackstone permitted himself a long look at Sierra as she stood behind her desk in shorts and a snow-white T-shirt – sapphire eyes, dark gold skin, the broad shoulders of a swimmer, the slender but perfectly muscled legs of a hiker and skier, a smile that was not afraid to smile even with Blackstone gazing at her. Finally he dropped himself onto one of the chairs in the waiting area.

"All right," he said. "Waiting has its consolations."

She sat down and went back to her computer. "Thank you, pastor."

"I didn't even know there was going to be a march by white supremacists."

"Tom kept it as quiet as he could."

"Where are they from?"

"Idaho."

"Good. They can go back to Idaho." He squirmed in his seat. "These chairs are pretty hard to relax in."

"Sorry. But you don't need to relax, do you, reverend? You only work one day a week."

Blackstone laughed. "We only had coffee once, Sierra Bloom, that doesn't mean you can sass me."

She lifted her blue eyes from the computer screen. "It was a long coffee."

"Not long enough."

"Ask me again. Maybe we can stretch it out for three or four hours."

"Really?"

"You won't know unless you ask."

Blackstone leaned forward in his chair. "That sounds like a challenge."

"Whatever works."

"Is it a bad line if I say your eyes make me think of the word *electricity*?"

"Not too shabby." Sierra was typing. "What else have you got?"

"How about when you smile my whole mind blanks out and I just think, *Wow, ignition*!"

She grinned but didn't raise her eyes. "*Ignition?* I've never heard that one before. You make me sound like a Harley Fat Boy."

"You might be a Harley but you're no Fat Boy."

"The gallant vicar. Isn't that what the British call you guys? Vicars?"

"It doesn't matter what the British call me, Sierra, what do you call me?"

"The Procrastinating Pastor. Are you going to ask me out again or not?"

"I was just getting to that but thinking of great pick up lines threw me off."

"A face and a heart like yours doesn't need great pick up lines." Her blue eyes went to the glass door and large glass windows. "Too late. Here's the man."

"Friday night?"

She darted a look in his direction. "Yes."

"Yes?"

The smile. And a light that moved quickly through her eyes. "Yes."

"Eight?"

"Oh, much sooner than that, vicar."

"Well, Reverend Blackstone." Tall and lean and wearing a slate gray Stetson, Sheriff Tom Youngblood came through the door. "You actually listened to Sierra and stayed put?"

"Looks that way."

"Guess I'll have to give her a raise."

"Whatever you need to do to keep her there. Otherwise I may have to hire her as my own secretary."

"Ha. Wouldn't that get Diamondback talking? Come on back. Sierra, if I'm not out in half an hour call the FBI satellite office in Missoula. Tell them to bring their best shooters to Diamondback in Blackhawks."

"Will do, chief."

As Blackstone followed the sheriff into his office he mouthed *seven* at Sierra and she mouthed back *five.*

"Close the door, will you, reverend?" Youngblood put his Stetson down on his desk, crown first. His hair was short and the color of fresh rust. "A little bit of a *hora* by 7-11."

"Hope Beth Shalom got the better of those Nazis."

"Yeah?" Youngblood sat in his swivel chair and put his feet up on the desk. He was wearing a khaki uniform and his cowboy boots were chocolate brown. "Rabbi Cohen's congregation was mostly chanting, *No Nazis, no way, God bless USA.* I suppose you would have come to blows with the white power advocates?"

"Hard to say."

"Hmm. A man of the cloth."

"Even Jesus flipped tables when it was necessary."

Youngblood hooked into Blackstone with his sharp gray eyes. "Are you carrying?"

"Of course I'm carrying. What's the use of a concealed weapon permit if I don't make use of it? For that matter, what's the use of the Second Amendment?"

8

"This is Montana, reverend. I don't need an NRA speech. Tell me again about the March shooting."

"Sheriff, I was cleared of any wrongdoing. It was self-defense."

"I know that. But tell me again."

"There was a cult committing murders in Diamondback. One of the leaders was a man from Helena who passed himself off as a minister. He ordered your predecessor, Sheriff Parker, to shoot me. I wrestled the sheriff's gun away from him – "

"The report says you broke his hand and that you did it with a very fast movement, like karate or something," interrupted Youngblood.

"Okay, I broke the sheriff's hand, and I did it quickly because I had maybe three seconds to live. I used his gun on the Satanist from Helena."

"See, this is where I have trouble. All the devil worship and cult stuff I can work my way through. Even though it makes no sense it still makes more sense than a Baptist minister acting like James Bond."

"I was in the military, sheriff."

"You were a navy chaplain."

"Sure, but they still taught us self-defense. Don't forget I served the Navy Seals. They're not going to listen to anything I have to say about the soul if they don't think I know what it means to get physical."

"So is that what you did, reverend? Got physical? Went on some special ops with Seal Team Six? Waxed some tangos?"

"That information's classified."

"Ha. I'll bet it is. A pistol packin' preacher. They say you didn't even blink when you shot the guy or have any sort of problems with it afterwards. No PTSD issues for you. Which tells me you've done it before." Youngblood paused a moment. "Those white supremacists have come to stay."

"What? Sierra said they were from Idaho."

"They were. But their name tells the story, doesn't it? Montana Justice Movement. I'm afraid they're settling in. They have an acreage out by Cayuse Flats. The old Reynolds' place."

"That's a big property."

Youngblood nodded. "I reckon they'll set up a compound. Those militia types always do."

Blackstone let out a long breath of air. "Great."

"There's more."

"What's more?"

"They're a bona fide church."

"According to who? God or the State?"

"The Feds. Reverend Matt Skeritt. About your age and build. Blond, blue-eyed, perfect Aryan."

"That's good to hear."

"You'd be a perfect Aryan too if your hair wasn't black."

"Glad I was spared the honor. Why are they here in Anaconda County, Tom? Why aren't they settling into a bigger center like Missoula?"

"Beats me. Guess they wanted more land and more privacy. Waco wasn't exactly the capital of Texas, but Branch Davidian liked it."

"Let's hope we don't wind up with another Branch Davidian."

"Let's hope. Anyway, that's not why I asked you to meet with me today." Youngblood picked up a pen from his desktop and tapped it against the dark wood. "My predecessor, may God have mercy on his soul, earmarked you for chaplaincy work with the Sheriff's Office. I don't know whether that was in order to keep a closer eye on you or what, but is that something I can still count on you to help me with when I ask?"

"Absolutely, Tom."

"The Catholic priest was on the list as well as a Father Daniel, Greek Orthodox, but he lives in Missoula."

"Missoula's only an hour's drive. And there's talk about him spearheading a new work here in Diamondback next year. Both of them would be assets to you."

"What about the rabbi?"

"John Cohen? Solid gold."

"I haven't had a chance to get to know the new Lutheran minister or the new pastor at Abundant Springs."

"Neither have I. They've only been here a couple of months. Maybe wait on them a bit."

Youngblood laid down the pen. "No word on when the Methodist church or Foursquare church are getting their new ministers?"

"No. I'm not even sure the United Methodists want to keep their church up. I've heard a rumor that another denomination, the Free Methodist Church, might be buying the building and starting its own ministry here in Anaconda County."

"Is that a good thing?"

"Sure, it's a good thing. They're a fine group of Christians."

"I wonder if I might ask my own pastor to be one of the chaplains?"

"That's totally your call. But Brett Sanders is well liked and Vineyard is an excellent fellowship. None of us would have a problem working with him."

"All right." Youngblood had fifteen years on Blackstone. He leaned back in his chair and studied the face of the thirty-two old minister. "One more question and I'm done. From the FBI reports on last winter's series of murders it sounds like a number of the pastors assisted with the investigation. From time to time they offered valuable insights and that includes your self."

"Right."

"I wonder how open you and a few of the other pastors might be to helping me along the same lines?"

"Why – " Blackstone tried to read the expression in the sheriff's eyes. "Of course. I know Father Eric and Father Daniel and Rabbi Cohen would want to assist in any way they could. But there's nothing serious going on right now, is there?"

"I've been turning this over ever since I got word about the Montana Justice Movement setting up shop here. There's going to be trouble, Jude. I can feel it in my bones." He jerked his head at the computer monitor on the left hand side of the desk. "I had a surveillance camera set up by the Reynolds' place. It's not on the property the MJM purchased, but I can see the main road and right into the acreage. Every time one of these militias moves into a county bad doings aren't far behind."

"Surveillance?" Blackstone was surprised. "Is that legal?"

The sheriff shrugged. "I say it is. When that feeling goes through me like a rattlesnake I've learned to pay attention. The camera is a precaution. You ever get those gut feelings, Jude?"

"Yeah. I get them."

"Got any now?"

"I do."

"Get any when you saw those Nazis marching down the street waving swastikas and shouting their filthy slogans?"

"Some."

Ten minutes later Blackstone parked in his spot next to Blue Sky Baptist Church. A vehicle he didn't recognize, a black Chevy Suburban, was parked nearby. It had Idaho plates and it was empty.

"Someone is waiting for me inside," he murmured as he climbed out of his jeep, "and they're from the same state as the white supremacists. Now my gut feeling is going into overdrive."

A blonde man was sitting in the small alcove just outside Blackstone's office. He was wearing a blue suit with matching tie and had a white silk handkerchief tucked into his breast pocket. He got up as Blackstone approached. The secretary, Crystal Jackson, had a large window in her office that allowed her to see everything that was going on in the church. She came towards Blackstone at the same time as the man in the blue suit.

"Pastor," she said, "this is Reverend Matt Skeritt. He's been waiting to see you."

"Pleased to meet you Pastor Blackstone." Skeritt extended his hand. "I've just arrived in Diamondback."

Blackstone took the hand. "Welcome. What church are you with, Reverend Skeritt?"

"Lord of Lords. We've purchased a building on the edge of town."

"Lord of Lords? What denomination is that?"

"We see ourselves as nondenominational, but we are affiliated with Christ the Supreme Redeemer. It's an international organization of churches."

"I've heard of that. Aren't they connected to The High Cross Christian Movement?"

Skeritt smiled. "You're well informed."

"Well, please join me in my office."

"You have marriage counseling in half an hour, Pastor Jude," Crystal reminded him. "Cliff Hardwick and Linda Smythe."

"I won't take up more than ten minutes of his time, don't worry," said Skeritt.

Blackstone sat behind his desk and Skeritt took a chair.

"I'm interested in the ministerial you hold here at Blue Sky Baptist," Skeritt told Blackstone. "I've heard it meets once a month."

"That's right," Blackstone replied. "Usually it's the first Wednesday of the month but we moved it to the week after due to a number of funerals several of the pastors had to take care of."

"So you're getting together next Wednesday at noon?"

"Yes."

"I'd like to join you, if I may."

"You realize there are two ministerials, Reverend Skeritt? Another meets at the Vineyard Fellowship, Anaconda Vineyard. Pastor Brett Sanders heads it up. He favors ten gallon hats."

"Anaconda Vineyard? That's an ominous name."

"Only if you're afraid of snakes."

Skeritt's blue eyes glittered and then went flat again. "Why are there two?"

"Brett's is more geared to evangelical churches – "

"That's us," interrupted Skeritt.

" – while the one here is open to all the Christian groups whether they consider themselves evangelical or not. In addition, we often have visits from clergy who serve other faiths. Buddhist, Muslim, Bahai – it's a way of building bridges. No one waters anything down. Christians still talk and pray like Christians. But such gatherings build trust and understanding rather than walls."

"I see. So anything goes?"

Blackstone shook his head. "No. New Age practitioners don't join us. Or witches. Or devil worshippers. We draw a line there."

"What about Jews?"

"Jews are welcome. Rabbi Cohen of Beth Shalom meets with us frequently. After all, Reverend Skeritt, Jesus was a Jew. Wouldn't you agree?"

Skeritt's eyes took on a hard-edged darkness.

Blackstone stared into that darkness and into the past.

Torches flamed in iron brackets mounted on long walls.

Nazi flags hung from poles between the torches, red and white with black swastikas.

Men and women were giving the stiff-armed Nazi salute and shouting, "Heil Hitler! Heil Satan! Heil White Christ!"

At the front of the hall with its high ceilings, several men in black SS uniforms had forced an older man in gray pants and a white shirt to his knees. Each of the SS officers pointed daggers at the man's head.

"Behold the Jew!" cried one of the officers.

"Behold the Deceiver of Mankind!" shouted the officer next to him.

"Behold the Blood Sacrifice that will appease our Lord Satan and the White Christ!" called out the third.

The officers began to chant in German, their voices rising. The hundreds assembled in brown pants and tunics, in high black boots and Sam Browne belts, shouted louder and louder until the din in the hall reached a crescendo.

"Strike!" the crowd of men and women finally screamed. "Strike!"

"Heil Hitler, strike!" shrieked the first SS officer, bending his arm back, the dagger in his fist flashing in the torchlight.

"Heil Satan, strike!" yelled the officer beside him.

"Heil White Christ, strike!" bellowed the third officer, his dagger poised to begin its downward slash.

No one heard the shots.

Blackstone knew the sniper rifles were silenced.

As if one bullet had felled them all, the three SS officers were hurled backwards across the stage they stood on.

The ten undercover agents among the crowd, five of them Israelis, the other five Jews from Berlin, tore off their brown tunics to reveal white shirts emblazoned with large blue Stars of David. They all held Uzis.

"Everyone on the floor!" the Jewish agents shouted. "Hands on your heads! You are under arrest!"

"If you try to escape you will be shot!" Blackstone heard several of the agents yell.

Dozens of people ran for the doors.

They found their way blocked by members of Germany's GSG 9 counter terrorist unit.

The GSG 9 police were dressed in black tactical uniforms.

Black helmets were on their heads. Their faces were shielded by dark visors.

Gloved hands held Heckler and Koch MP5 machine pistols.

Several of the Nazis still pulled out handguns from leather holsters.

They were shot within seconds, the crash of the HK automatic weapons blasting off the ceiling and walls.

"Runter oder sterben!" barked one of the GSG 9 commanders.

Get down or die!

The men and women who had been rushing the doors instantly dropped to the floor.

Blackstone, dressed in a brown uniform with Sam Browne belt like the other undercover agents, had been standing at attention under a portrait of Adolf Hitler. Now he had a SIG P228 pointed at a bearded man who appeared to be holding a grenade.

"Don't attempt to prime it," Blackstone said in English.

The man looked at him and at the extended magazine that protruded from the grip of Blackstone's 9mm handgun. But he continued to toy with the grenade.

Blackstone shook his head. "I will put twenty bullets into your brain."

The man stared.

"Zwanzig." Blackstone repeated the number in German.

Then he began to count. "Eins, zwei, drei . . . "

The man quickly gave Blackstone the grenade and lay down on the floor, interlacing his fingers at the back of his head.

"Danke," Blackstone said to him.

"Schwein," the man growled.

"Jesus is a Hebrew." Skeritt's eyes remained dark. "A white man with an Indo-European Aryan bloodline."

"Really? Born in Bethlehem to Jewish parents both of the line of David, the great King of Israel in 1000 BC? How did he pull that one off?"

"His father was not Joseph, was it? His father was God Almighty. And God Almighty is holy. He is white and pure as snow. And man and woman created in his image are the same. The others are *untermensch*, slaves that

Aryans were destined to rule. Only then is the world in perfect synch."

"Salvation is from the Jews, Reverend Skeritt. Jesus – pardon me, Yeshua – it was he who said that."

"An aberrant text. A gloss added by a Jew."

"I've never seen information like that pop up in my studies of the Greek New Testament."

"This Rabbi Cohen of yours, he will not attend the other ministerial, will he?"

"Not to my knowledge. Though Brett wouldn't kick him out if he did show up. Brett's a strong supporter of the State of Israel and the Jewish people in general. Not that he doesn't pray for the Arabs or Palestinians. After all, they are the children of Ishmael, of the lineage of Abraham, the father of the Jews, and God promised he would make of Ishmael's bloodline a great nation as well."

"I need to be on my way." Skeritt got to his feet.

"Auschwitz calling?"

"I wish to God it were. That's a shrine to us."

"I'm not surprised. Crypts and human slaughter have always attracted devil worshippers."

Skeritt half-laughed. "Devil worshippers? Are we on the set of *Rosemary's Baby*?"

"The High Cross Christian Movement has connections to *Zabolus*. And *Zabolus* is a secret society steeped in Satan worship and the Black Mass from at least 700 AD."

"That's a legend. It's never been proven in a court of law."

"I don't care about human courts when it comes to the supernatural and the diabolical, Reverend Skeritt. And neither do you."

Skeritt smirked. "I'll crush you, Blackstone. I'll grind you down into a fine powder, mix you in a cup of human blood, and pour you onto the black altar as a perfect sacrifice to our Lord of Lords."

"Not if you lose your life first, Skeritt, your life and your soul."

The two men's blue eyes came together like fists.

"You could give your life to Christ and live forever," said Blackstone quietly. "No hellfire. No damnation."

"I have given my life to Christ, the White Christ."

"You've given your life to the Beast. Switch allegiances, Skeritt. Worship the true God. It's not too late."

"What? Bow down to a weakling who died on a cross like a common criminal instead of leading a revolt and conquering Rome? No, Blackstone, I kneel before the White Christ who never died on a cross of shame. The White Christ brought Almighty God and Lord Satan together as one in his body and spirit, he married heaven and hell. Then he brought this truth and power to Europe, to what Rome called Magna Germania, where he took a German wife and bore German children. His offspring are still among us. Think of that, Blackstone. The children of Christ's children are still among us. We know who they are and we guard them well, oh, *Heil the White Christ*! We guard them well."

"You can't be serious, Skeritt."

"I'm serious as hell, Blackstone." Skeritt turned as he opened the door. "Think it over. It's you who should be planning on switching allegiances. I could put you in the same room as a blood son of Christ. The man wields enormous wealth and influence. The IMF and EU and The Inner Six do his bidding. At his word nations rise and fall. He could turn your life right side up, Blackstone. He could make you a god."

2

Blackstone was doing a morning run when Beth Shalom synagogue blew up.

He was on a ridge overlooking the city of Diamondback and had just made up his mind to sprint the next two hundred yards when a fireball burst on his eyes. He stopped and removed his sunglasses. Orange flames were shooting hundreds of feet into the air. After a few seconds a loud *WHUMP* reached his ears and a shock wave of hot air slapped him in the face. He knew it was the synagogue because for a moment he recognized the roof and the trees and the road that curved past the property. Then everything was a flash of orange and yellow and white.

He ran down from the ridge and raced towards the fire. First responders were already there when he reached what was left of the synagogue. A firefighter ordered him to stay back.

"It's a torch," the fireman warned. "You can see how fast it's burning. In twenty minutes there won't be a thing left."

"Was anyone in there?" demanded Blackstone. "Were the rabbi or any of his people in the synagogue?"

"I don't know, sir, but you need to stay well back. For all we know there could be a second explosion."

"How did it start? Do you have any idea?"

"Not right now we don't. Give us some time."

A minute later Rabbi Cohen came to a screeching stop in his dark blue van. Blackstone fired off a prayer of thanks and was at the rabbi's side the moment he jumped out onto the street.

"John, I'm sorry," said Blackstone.

"What started it? Is anyone in there?"

"I don't know."

Cohen ran towards the blaze. Two firefighters sprang on him and held him back. His black fedora flew from his head.

"I'm the rabbi!" he protested. "That's my synagogue!"

"There's nothing you can do," a tall firefighter told him. "It's gone."

"But there could be someone in there, the janitor, or one of our leaders."

"No one can go into that fire, sir. It's an inferno."

"How did it start?"

"Witnesses say there was an explosion. Maybe there was a gas leak. It's too soon to say. I'm sorry."

Cohen put his hat back on his head and hung back, watching the firefighters play their hoses over the sharp flames. Blackstone stood beside him. Cohen rubbed his fingers anxiously over the closely trimmed beard on his jaw, moving them back and forth as the synagogue disappeared in smoke and fire.

"I can't imagine what could have happened," he murmured. "Something electrical? A candle? But I was here till eleven last night. Everything was fine. I swear it."

"They'll go through what's left, John," Blackstone said. "They'll be able to tell where the source of the fire was."

"I pray the synagogue was empty, Jude."

"So do I."

No one was in Beth Shalom when it burned to the ground. To the relief of everyone from the synagogue, and the churches, and the neighborhood, the firefighters did not find any bodies when they went through the blackened timbers and the ashes. But neither did they find any clues to the cause of the blaze, not in the hours after the fire was extinguished or in the days that followed.

"Look, you don't have to share this with your people." Sheriff Youngblood sat facing Cohen and Blackstone in his office. "In fact, I'd rather you didn't. I suppose the rumors will start making their way through Anaconda County soon enough, but until then you ought to keep a lid on what I'm about to tell you."

"It was arson." Cohen's face was without expression. "Wasn't it? Not faulty wiring?"

"Yes. Arson."

Cohen's face remained emotionless.

Blackstone glanced at his friend. *The long hard journey of the Jews.*

"Who?" asked Cohen. "How?"

"I can't answer either of those questions," replied the sheriff. "Neither can the fire chief. Neither can the experts who drove in from Missoula and Denver. There's no trace of a bomb, no ruptured gas line, no wiring issues, no evidence of a fire starting up from any location whatsoever. It's as if your synagogue was hit by an instant and massive flashover with no obvious source. As if fire dropped out of the sky and engulfed the building all at once, not from the roof down, not from the ground up, just an instant conflagration hitting every part of the synagogue at the same time."

What Blackstone called his Iceman walked up and down his spine. "That doesn't sound natural, sheriff."

"No, it doesn't. I'm sure there's a logical explanation. It's just escaped everyone so far."

"What about the Montana Justice Movement?" asked Blackstone. "What about Skeritt and his Lord of Lords church?"

"We've had them under surveillance. Absolutely nothing was happening at their property the night before Beth Shalom went up in flames. No vehicles came or went and that's true of the morning the synagogue exploded as well."

"What about the cameras on the street in front of Beth Shalom?" demanded Cohen. "What do they tell you?"

"Two of them were incinerated in the blast. Footage from the third shows no one and nothing. We see you leave about eleven at night. Everything's quiet. The sun comes up. Then the synagogue is a fireball." Youngblood snapped his fingers. "Just like that."

The rabbi shook his head. "It makes no sense."

"No, it doesn't." Youngblood shot Blackstone a look. "Well?"

"Well what?"

"Are you going to give me a hocus pocus explanation?"

"A hocus pocus explanation?"

"The devil? Witches? Broomsticks? Black Sabbaths?"

"You know Skeritt's church is connected to the High Cross Christian Movement?"

"So?"

"So spend a few minutes and Google it. They're rabidly anti-Jewish. Members have been charged with desecrating Jewish tombstones and synagogues in Europe. They've even been accused of beating an elderly rabbi and gang raping Jewish women."

"Have the charges stuck?"

"Their lawyers are diabolical."

Youngblood snorted. "I thought most lawyers were diabolical."

"Theirs are even more diabolical than is usually the case. You ought to drive out to the MJM property and ask a few questions, sheriff."

"Why bother? We don't have anything on them."

"Just watch their eyes. See what their eyes tell you."

"What do you think they'll tell me?"

Blackstone half-smiled. "If your questions are provocative they'll tell you a lot."

"Hm. Can you give me an idea of a suitably provocative question for a pack of neo-Nazis, pastor?"

"Tell them you don't believe the fire fell from the sky. Tell them you think it swarmed up from the pit."

"Swarmed up from the pit. You mean like them?"

Blackstone nodded as Iceman did another of his cold walks. "Exactly like them."

"I may not need to add that little bit."

"Just suggest a supernatural explanation for the fire. And see what happens."

"Do you think they're going to become fireballs too?"

"I think," replied Blackstone, "you're going to see a wicked delight in their eyes, maybe even on their faces, if they don't check themselves quickly enough."

"And what does wicked delight look like?"

"You'll know. There won't be any problem picking up on that."

"Is this going to be hocus pocus stuff, Jude?"

Blackstone shrugged. "After a while human evil and supernatural evil begin to look one and the same."

High Mountain Grill & Steakhouse
That evening

"Jude."

"Hmm?"

"You're not with me."

"How could I not be with you? I'm sitting right across from you and you look incredible."

"Don't change the subject by running to my looks. Your head is in the clouds. Do you mind if I join you there? Or is someone else ahead of me?"

"It's just work stuff, Sierra. It's not interesting."

"I'm interested in your work stuff. Aren't we trying to build a relationship here?"

Blackstone let out a lungful of air. He used a steak knife to trace a quick pattern in the spilled salt by his plate. "What does your boss tell you about the Beth Shalom fire?"

"Sheriff Youngblood? He says there's a simple explanation, so simple it's evaded everyone up to this point."

"What do you think?"

Sierra's rich blue eyes widened. "Me? So you're finally asking the expert?"

"I am."

"Someone came to a service and left a device behind under one of the seats, you know, something out of sight that would stick to the bottom of a chair or pew."

"If that's so why isn't there any trace of it? A timer or part of a metal or plastic casing?"

"The fire wiped it out."

"But they found segments of Torah scrolls. Shoes and slippers Rabbi Cohen left in his office. Even a charred picture of his wife and kids. But no evidence of a bomb or incendiary device like you suggest."

Sierra folded her hands under her chin, elbows on the table. "I love this."

"What?"

"Being in the clouds with you."

"I wish the clouds weren't so gray."

"That's okay. I can handle it." Sierra's eyes became a deep indigo. "Sheriff Youngblood told me about your real theories."

"Did he? And what are they?"

"I Googled Lord of Lords. They have a sharp website. Kind of cover up their neo-Nazi stuff with pictures of clean cut All American families and the Rockies and the building that serves as their church. Somebody put together a pretty fancy pile of logs, Jude."

"It came with the farm."

"They say a lot of patriotic things. Have pictures of Jesus and Reverend Skeritt in a suit. American flag. USMC flag. Bald eagles. You know."

"Any links?"

"Not to hell. But I looked for the High Cross Christian Movement on my own. Their site was a lot more intense. Beautiful photographs, very classy and professional, but not geared for the general viewer. It was all for their own blood. And for seekers."

"So what do you think?"

"I think they're serious. And I think there's a lot more to it. Are you going to share what you know with me?"

Blackstone waited while the waitress refilled his coffee and offered Sierra another pot of chamomile tea.

"How long have we known each other?" asked Blackstone, sipping his coffee.

She shrugged her shoulders under her sleeveless white T-shirt. "I've been here since June."

"All the way from Aspen. And I met you when?"

She grinned. "You came by to protest a parking fine. I wouldn't let you see Sheriff Youngblood or any of the deputies. I said it was a trivial matter and not worth their time."

"And what did I do?"

"You laughed and left. If I 'd known you were going to sit on the hood of the sheriff's patrol car till he came out I would have followed you outside and run you off."

"To tell you the truth, I was kind of hoping you'd do something like that."

"Oh, you hardly even noticed me, Jude, you were so annoyed about the ticket. It was all of what, five bucks?"

"Fifty bucks. And I noticed you all right."

"Really? What was I wearing?"

"Faded jeans. Wide belt with nickel studs. Hiking boots with Vibram soles. Sky blue Patagonia top. Levi jacket without sleeves. I don't think you like sleeves. And you had blue turquoise earrings."

Sierra stopped pouring her tea. "Are you kidding me?"

"I thought you were the most beautiful thing I'd seen in Montana. You made the Rockies look like a bad idea." Blackstone smiled and leaned back in his seat. "But you never came through the doors. Tom Youngblood did. Big disappointment. He knocked twenty-five bucks off my ticket though."

Sierra stirred honey into her cup of herbal tea. "If it was love at first sight why did it take you so long to come back and harass me?"

"Holidays started the next day. I headed north of the 49th to Waterton Lakes and Banff and Jasper in Alberta. Hiked and took pictures and slept under the stars with grizzlies."

"I'll bet." She spent a few moments looking at his face. "You're a handsome creature, Pastor Jude. I wish you'd take me up into those mountains of yours someday soon. I'd feel safe sleeping under the stars if you were there."

"No can do. People would talk. It would look bad."

"Maybe we can start with a day hike."

"I think we can."

She reached across the table for his hand and curled her strong tanned fingers around it. "I don't mind you being a pastor, you know, a holy man. But there's a lot more to you than that. Or the quality of seminary grads is going way, way up."

"Probably a little of both."

Her finger ran up and down his wrist. "I kind of have a crush on you."

"That's good to hear."

"I'm thinking of switching to your church."

"Don't do that."

She looked hurt, her lips coming together in a pout. "Why not?"

"Four reasons. Brett Sanders will accuse me of sheep stealing. You'll break every single man's heart at Anaconda Vineyard. And the Beth Shalom congregation that meets there on Friday night, Erev Shabbat, and on Saturday morning, they count on you to sing for them."

"I can still sing for them, Jude. Your services are on Sunday mornings and evenings."

"How did you learn to sing in Hebrew like that? You never told me."

Sierra rested her chin on one hand. "I lived in Israel. Kibbutz Hatzor. Right by Hatzor Air Force Base. I worked in the *pardes* mostly, the orchard. I learned Hebrew and Arabic while I was there. I started doing songs for Shabbat when Uri overheard me singing to myself way off in the far corner of the grapefruit orchard, you know, *eshkalot.*" She lifted her fingers from his hand a moment and made a twisting motion as if she were picking a grapefruit. "My voice is not such a big deal."

"No, not at all, you only sound like Celine Dion."

Her cheeks flushed rose. "I do not. You and your lines."

"I could listen to you all day and all night."

The rose color darkened. "What's number four?"

"Number four?"

"You always pay me all these compliments and distract us from what we were talking about. What's the fourth reason I can't come to the Baptist church?"

"Me."

"You? I thought you liked the girl named Sierra Bloom."

"Just a bit."

"So?"

"So do you honestly think I could concentrate on my message with you sitting there staring at me with those blue sky eyes? I'd probably start babbling about the Song of Solomon."

"Oh, the Song of Solomon is very romantic; I wouldn't mind that."

"The rest of the church might wonder about the sudden shift."

"Tell them you had a word of knowledge."

Blackstone laughed. "You really are funny."

Her hand was still on his. "Can we go for a walk or something? Down by the river?"

Blackstone finished his coffee. "Sure can."

His cellphone went off.

Brass instruments blared.

Shirley Bassey began to belt out *Goldfinger*.

She gave him a face. "James Bond?"

"That's me."

"So I'm what? A Bond girl?"

"You nailed it. Just a sec." Blackstone spoke into his cell. "Pastor Jude here."

"Jude? Brett Sanders."

"Brett? We were just talking about you."

Sierra made another face.

"I hope it was good, Jude."

"All good."

"I don't want to keep you. I just have a prayer request. That Skeritt guy showed up at the ministerial at Vineyard today."

"Oh oh. Was he trouble?"

"No. All silk and smiles. Everyone liked him."

"Really?"

"Really. And that's what I want prayer for. The guy somehow got into everybody's headspace and worked all of us around to his way of thinking."

"About what?"

"Everything. Jews. Jesus going from Israel to Magna Germania and siring children. The importance of the white race in God's eyes. It made so much sense I never argued. No one did. It wasn't until a couple of hours later that I seemed to shake the cobwebs loose."

"What are you saying? Do you think he put you under a spell or something?"

Sierra's dark gold eyebrows arched.

"Maybe he put something in the coffee. Maybe he sprinkled black magic on the donuts. All I know is the other pastors still think he's the greatest thing since the New Testament."

"No way."

"I called through the list before I hit speed dial for you. They're singing his praises. Want to take him up on his offer to have a ministerial next week at Lord of Lords."

"Didn't you argue with them?"

"Oh, yeah."

"And?"

"And they quoted verses back at me until I went deaf, call after call after call. They had some kind of weird logic I couldn't refute. It was all over the map but it made perfect sense. So I'm asking you to pray. Pray with all your heart and soul. Something's in the air and it's too strong for flesh and blood."

"Did the men decide to go to Lord of Lords?"

"That's up in the air too."

Blackstone ended the call. He glanced across the table at Sierra.

"Well?" she asked.

Light came through the café window and got caught up in her golden hair and azure eyes.

"Say something," she demanded. "What's going on?"

"I was going to say you look bewitching. But that's not appropriate." Blackstone put a twenty on the table. "You still want that walk by the river?"

"Absolutely."

They both got up at the same time. His eyes stayed on hers.

"Do you want a dolls and daffodils walk?" he asked. "Or do you want to know about the phone call?"

Her eyes turned gray and narrowed. "Can't we have both?"

"No."

She hesitated. "You said something about Pastor Brett being put under a spell."

"The phone call it is."

The two of them left the café and walked down the street together.

"So what have I chosen in place of romance?" asked Sierra.

"The devil and all his works."

Jude Blackstone's house
Friday night
Erev Shabbat

Blackstone sat very still in a Morris chair he had placed in the middle of his living room. His eyes were closed.

He was thinking in Hebrew, German, Latin, and Greek.

But when he spoke out loud it was in English.

"Christ, clear my head. Christ, clear my eyes. Christ, clear my spirit."

He paused.

"And clear the heads, eyes, and spirits of my brothers."

He began to recite a passage of scripture in Latin.

De cetero, fratres, confortamini in Domino, et in potentia virtutis ejus.

One part of his mind put the words in a loose English translation of his own as he spoke the Latin.

Brothers, be strong in the Lord. Be strong in his mighty power.

Induite vos armaturam Dei, ut possitis stare adversus insidias diaboli.

Put God's body armor on. All of it. That way you'll be able to make a stand against the devil's wicked ways.

Quoniam non est nobis colluctatio adversus carnem et sanguinem, sed adversus principes, et potestates, adversus mundi rectores tenebrarum harum, contra spiritualia nequitiæ, in cælestibus.

Our fight is not with enemies of flesh and blood. It is with evil wielded by men of power and spirits of power from an unseen world. It is with wicked creatures of the Great Darkness. It is with hellfire;it is with grotesque angels in the realms of the damned.

Propterea accipite armaturam Dei, ut possitis resistere in die malo, et in omnibus perfecti stare.

Put all the body armor on so you can defy the enemy in the hour of evil. Make sure you are the last man standing.

State ergo succincti lumbos vestros in veritate, et induti loricam justitiæ, et calceati pedes in præparatione Evangelii pacis, in omnibus sumentes scutum fidei, in quo possitis omnia tela nequissimi ignea extinguere.

Stand your ground. Your tactical belt is the hard truth. Your body armor is the power of God. Your boots are the strong peace of the strong news of Christ's Crucifixion and Resurrection and the release of the hostages. Your riot shield will block all the incendiaries of hell.

Et galeam salutis assumite, et gladium spiritus (quod est verbum Dei), per omnem orationem et obsecrationem orantes omni tempore in spiritu: et in ipso vigilantes in omni instantia et obsecratione pro omnibus sanctis.

Your helmet protects your head and your mind. Your weapon is God's Spirit and God's words. Never stop praying. Do it everywhere. Be alert. Always go armed. Always go in faith. Always have the back of all Christ's people.

Blackstone opened his eyes.

"Saint Michael," he whispered, "Servant of the Most High God, Archangel, defend us in battle. Be our defense against the wickedness and snares of the devil. May God rebuke him, we humbly pray. And you, Prince of the heavenly host, by the power of God, thrust into hell Satan and the other evil spirits who prowl the world for the ruin of souls. Amen, let it be so."

He continued to sit quietly. Then he began another prayer.

"My Lord and my God," he started out.

The room blazed with white light.

He threw his arm over his eyes and cringed in his chair.

"There is nothing to fear." The voice was everywhere. It resonated in his brain and in his soul and made the air in the room burn.

"Michael," he whispered.

His mind filled with a vision of Sierra standing in a simple blue cotton dress and singing an Erev Shabbat song. Candles flamed and made her waver in their light. Faces were turned towards her. He saw Rabbi Cohen. All the men wore black *kippas* on their heads and the women scarves.

Her song was beautiful and brought peace to the hard beating of his heart.

But suddenly the candle flames burst into monstrous fires.

Women screamed as their dresses caught. Men tried to smother the flames with their suit jackets but their hands turned into torches. Then their faces and mouths and eyes.

For an instant Blackstone had an image of a crematorium, bodies heaped inside, smoke pouring from a tall brick chimney.

Then Sierra fell, a swirling mass of black and red flames.

The light vanished from the room.

Blackstone stumbled out the front door of his house, trying to call Rabbi Cohen on his cellphone. The rabbi didn't answer. Neither did Sierra.

They don't have their phones on. Why would they? They're worshipping. She's singing. Perhaps John's already reading from the scrolls.

Or they're dead.

He punched the numbers 911.

"There's a fire at Anaconda Vineyard," he said, getting behind the wheel of his jeep.

"Who's calling, please? What's your name?"

"Anaconda Vineyard is an inferno. Get all the fire crews out."

Blackstone ended the call and began to drive. Soon he was going over a hundred miles an hour.

He speed dialed Brett Sanders.

"Pastor Sanders here."

"Brett. It's Jude. Your church is going up in flames."

"What? What are you talking about?"

"They've gone after the Vineyard church because you opened your doors to the Jews. Get there fast."

He turned his cell off.

He needed both hands and a focused mind to beat the devil to the Vineyard Fellowship.

How much time do I have, Lord?

Or is it already over?

I feel like you've given me time, enough time, if I can be fast enough.

At least as much time as you gave Joseph to save you and your mother when the soldiers were swarming down the road to Bethlehem, swords bared.

He gave the jeep more gas. The needle of the speedometer swung to one hundred and twenty. He kept to the main streets. Streetlights and stoplights streaked past. Cars and trucks were fast blurs. A siren began to wail. Then another. Red and blue and white flashed in his rearview mirror.

"That's fine," he muttered between teeth clenched so tightly his jaw ached. "Catch me if you can."

3

Blackstone's jeep screamed into the parking lot of Anaconda Vineyard.

Nothing was burning. There was no sign of flame.

But in his gut he knew it would all change within minutes.

He ran towards the building just as three patrol cars shrieked to a stop in front of him. He darted past them but Hal Gibson, a deputy Blackstone had shot skeet with the month before, blocked his path.

"Have you gone loco, Jude?" he demanded. "Calling in a fire when there ain't no fire? We traced your cell."

"No time, Hal."

Blackstone tried to move past Gibson but the huge deputy seized his arm. "Let go," Blackstone snapped.

"Not a chance. You're under arrest, preacher. You think you got one law and the rest of Anaconda County another? I'm throwing you in jail until you – "

Blackstone grabbed the deputy's arm and swung him over his hip onto the hood of the patrol car. Gibson cried out as he crashed into the metal and through the windshield. The other deputies were yanking out their handguns as Blackstone hurled himself through the doors and into the church.

Sierra was still singing. He could hear her voice through the mesquite doors that led into the sanctuary.

In his head and spirit were the flames.

He pulled the handle of the fire alarm in the hall.

A shrill warning began to sound in bursts of three.

He pushed through the mesquite doors.

"FIRE!" he shouted as loudly as he could. "EVERYONE OUT! FIRE!"

Sierra stopped singing and froze.

She stared at him as if he had lost his mind.

Even Rabbi Cohen jumped and looked at him in a way that told Blackstone he was not getting through despite the frantic beeping of the alarm.

He drew out his HK handgun from its concealed holster under the waistband of his jeans, pointed it at the ceiling, and began to shoot.

"Get out! Get out!"

He hadn't meant to shoot out lights but that's what happened.

Glass shattered and spun through the air and crashed onto the carpet.

Now women screamed and men hollered.

Blackstone got out of the way, putting his back against the wall, and continuing to shoot.

People roared up the center aisle and out the doors.

Blazing numerals were in his mind.

17, 16, 15, 14 . . .

"Are you crazy?" Sierra was in front of him. "You could kill someone! You're taking this demon hunting too far!"

She slapped him across the face as hard as she could.

Blackstone tasted the blood on his lip.

She clawed his arm, trying to reach the gun and pull it out of his hand.

She had strength. A lot of it. Too much for him to be gentle.

He threw his shoulder into Sierra, knocking the wind out of her stomach, slung her over his shoulder, and ran out of the church. He burst through the doors into the parking lot. Six deputies and Sheriff Youngblood had their pistols on him. They could not shoot because of Sierra.

"Throw down your gun!" barked Youngblood.

Blackstone tossed the HK towards him.

A wall of flame erupted in his head.

"Zero," he said, looking straight at Youngblood and his Glock.

The church exploded.

The blast knocked him flat.

He tucked Sierra's head into his shoulder and cushioned it so it would not be smacked against the pavement. He took the blow with his body.

Fire trucks streamed into the parking lot. He saw booted feet and yards of hose suddenly swelling with water. Heat made it feel like his skin was blistering. Someone took Sierra away from him. Someone else was snapping cuffs on his wrists.

"You're real scum." It was Hal Gibson. "Set it up like you did at Beth Shalom. Blew everything to kingdom come. Now you try to look like the Good Samaritan and haul everyone out of the building. You think no one will suspect. But we've got you, perp. You knew the church was going to go up. You even knew when."

"Get the dirt bag out of here," Blackstone heard Youngblood snarl. "Lock him up good and tight and throw the key down the toilet. He can crawl in after it if he wants it bad enough."

The sharp toe of cowboy boot drove into the side of his head and Blackstone was gone.

He opened his eyes in a cell.

"Want coffee?"

It was Gibson again.

Blackstone sat up on his cot.

Gibson grinned through his black beard, put his hand through the bars, and poured a cup of coffee on the concrete floor of the cell. Steam rose.

"There ya are, reverend," Gibson snorted. "You can get down on your hands and knees and lap it up."

"Where's Youngblood?" asked Blackstone.

"He don't wanna see you. And he's not in."

"Where's Sierra?"

"She don't wanna see you neither."

"What about the rabbi?"

"The rabbi? He'll never be by to talk to a Jew hater like you. You've burned all your bridges, preacher. You'd be better off if you'd let the church go up with everyone in it. Then we'd never have put two and two together. But you had an attack of conscience, didn't you? You're not much of a terrorist."

"I didn't start that fire. No human did."

"What? It was an act of God?"

"Not any god you'd know much about, Gibson."

"Oh, I get it, you're gonna play the hocus pocus card like you did last winter with Sheriff Parker. It won't work with the new team, preacher. If our five senses don't pick it up, it ain't real; it never was real. You set the explosives."

"You won't find any more trace of explosives in the ashes of Anaconda Vineyard than you did in the ashes of Beth Shalom, deputy."

"You're using some kind of new device. So what? Circumstantial evidence is enough to put you away for life."

"Hal." Sierra opened the steel door that led into the cellblock. "Jude has a visitor."

"No visitors, no way, Sherriff Youngblood's orders."

"He has a lawyer with him and the lawyer's threatening to bring in the Feds."

Gibson tugged at the closely trimmed beard on his jaw. "Five minutes."

She stepped aside.

Gibson grinned at Blackstone. "See? She won't even look at you. Only a day ago you had her eating out of your hand. Now you're dog scat."

Matt Skeritt, blonde and blue eyed, came into the corridor with a tall, thin man dressed in an impeccable black pinstripe suit, a dark goatee on his chin, his hair brushed back.

"Pastor Blackstone." Skeritt stopped in front of the cell. "This is Tony Evetts. He's an attorney from Helena. He'll arrange for your release."

"I have a lawyer," Blackstone replied.

"Where is he?"

"I just woke up. I haven't called him."

"The word I have is your lawyer won't take your case."

"My case? What case?"

"They're thinking of hanging terrorism charges on you."

Blackstone got up. "That so, Hal?"

Gibson nodded. "We're sure fire gonna try. The prosecutor's ready to take it on."

"Have I been out for two weeks? You had all that lined up already?"

"It's just about midnight. Yeah, we've been busy, preacher."

"It's midnight and you and Sierra are still here?"

43

"You bet. The witching hour. We don't want you flying away on us."

"The witching hour is three in the morning." Blackstone was looking at Skeritt and Evetts when he said it.

Evetts kept his gaze steady. "I'm your get out of jail free card."

Skeritt smiled. "You want to walk or not, Blackstone?"

"They can't keep you here, Reverend Blackstone." Evetts' voice was dark and dry. "They have no proof you set the fire at the church. All they can say is your hunch Anaconda Vineyard was the next target of the arsonists was based on the fact you planted the bomb. But that's conjecture. There's no hard evidence. Nothing the Sheriff's Office has will hold up in court. Unless they plant something that leads back to you. Some police like to work that way and be judge, jury, and executioner. But I can protect you from that. I have a high success rate defending men such as yourself from hillbilly sheriffs and backwater deputies and redneck prosecutors."

"I see. So I sign on to the white power movement and all's well in my little world?"

"A lot better than it is now." Skeritt gripped one of the bars. "Your chance to join the winning team, Blackstone. A whole thunderstorm is coming down over the next few days and weeks. It would be best if you stood under our roof."

"And if I don't?"

"You'll lose your soul. And everything that goes with it."

"I'll pass."

"You can't do anything without our help, Blackstone."

"I'll pass."

Skeritt dropped his voice so that the deputy would not hear him. "You understand what's going on, Blackstone. I have no idea what your background is; you don't show up on any of our high-end search engines, but you know who we are and you know what we do. The charm is working; you can see that. It's working on the pastors and it's working on the sheriff and his deputies and it's even working on that pretty girlfriend of yours."

"You won't get through to me, Skeritt."

"I believe you. We've tried and we're not going to expend any more effort in that direction. But we don't have to, do we? If everyone else is coming over to our side we don't have to worry about you. The opposite is actually true – you need to be worried about us and you need to be worried about yourself and you need to be worried about the people of Diamondback."

"Not too worried."

"Your few prayers against our hundreds of incantations? I beg to differ. Time to ramp up the worry, Blackstone."

"You first."

"Me?"

"God's going to work you over so hard your best friends in the Reichstag and the Illuminati won't recognize you."

"Really?" Skeritt laughed and raised his voice. "The sheriff is right about one thing – you are crazy. *Hasta la vista,* preacher. You're in for one of those dark nights of the soul you Christians seem to favor."

Skeritt and Evetts left through the steel door.

"Why didn't you take them up on their offer?" Gibson was puzzled. "You like bars and concrete for home décor?"

Blackstone sat back on his cot. "Skeritt's not my type. Neither is his cadaverous friend."

"His what?"

"Is it true what you said about my lawyer?"

"That he doesn't want anything to do with you? Yeah."

"Okay. I'll pray it over and decide who to call in the morning."

"You still praying?" Gibson hitched up his gun belt. "Well, I guess you don't have much else to work with."

"Not much else, no. Can I get a glass of water?"

"Fresh out of water. How about some Agent Orange?"

"Oh, Hal." Sierra came through the door with a styrofoam cup in her hand. "He can have a drop of water, for heaven's sakes. Go on, get out of here; I want a moment alone."

"I can't leave you all by yourself with Blackstone."

"What's he going to do? Squeeze between the bars? Go on, get; I need to tear a strip off him and I can't do it properly with you hanging on every word."

Gibson shook his head, but went back through the door.

Sierra handed the cup to Blackstone through the bars.

"Are you a mind reader?" asked Blackstone gulping it down. "You brought it just as I was asking Gibson for some."

"No mind reader. Just thoughtful."

"So no hocus pocus."

"No." There was a steel bench bolted to the floor in the corridor. She sat on it. "What's going on, Jude?"

"What's your take on it?"

She was still wearing her blue dress, the one she had sung the Erev Shabbat songs in. Her tanned shoulders were bare. She lifted them in a shrug.

"They say you had to have planted some sort of incendiary device. You knew where and when it was going to go off."

"Why didn't I just let it go off then? Why show up with a minute to spare and frighten everyone out of the building?"

"To make it look like you were innocent."

"Why would I need to do that? No one would have pointed the finger at me anyways."

"You decided you didn't want to kill all those people."

"At the last minute? A hardened killer like me suddenly experiences pangs of guilt and races across town to save the life of the woman he loves along with two hundred innocent souls?"

Sierra did not respond for several moments. "Is that what I am?"

Blackstone wrapped his hands around two of the bars. "Do you have a headache?"

"Is that your answer?" She made a sour face. "If I do it's probably due to the way you roughed me up in the church."

"Except."

"Except what?"

"Except Sheriff Youngblood and the deputies have headaches too."

She pinched her dark gold eyebrows together. "Gibson told you."

"Gibson was too busy harassing me to say anything about migraines."

"We don't have migraines."

"You will in the morning. Advil and Tylenol won't touch it, not even Tylenol 3."

"It's just a mix of stress and fatigue, Jude. You put us through the wringer tonight."

"Someone else will be putting you through the wringer between now and dawn."

"Oh, your devil stuff, I suppose. Nobody in the Sheriff's Office believes in all your abracadabra."

Blackstone's eyes stayed on hers. "Nobody?"

"Nobody. Even after our talk by the river the other evening. Look, I know as a pastor you think you need to believe in certain things. That's fine with me. Astronomers believe in stuff most of us haven't the faintest idea about. But I can't go there with you. Not tonight. Probably not ever."

"About noon the migraines will pass and you'll feel wonderful. All of you will. The whole city will. Tomorrow's Shabbat. I don't know where the Jewish congregation will be meeting – "

"I do, but I'm not supposed to tell you," Sierra broke in. "You might smuggle a message out to your team of arsonists."

" – but wherever they go there will be another attack."

"By your men?"

"Not by any men."

"So there will be another fire? I'll call the rabbi and tell him to change locations."

"It doesn't matter where he goes. The fire will follow him and his congregation."

"Then they can meet outside. Under the trees."

"The trees will burst into flames."

"Out in the open air then."

"The air will burn like a match."

"Oh, I don't believe you." She got to her feet. "I'm going home to get some sleep. And pop a couple of Ibuprofen."

"It won't help. And you won't get any sleep."

"Why not? Because the Nazis have put a spell on us?"

"Yes."

"And what's the cure for that spell?"

"Worship. As much worship of Jesus as you can put together. When you're pacing the floor an hour from now, and it feels like a metal band is being cranked tighter and tighter around your skull, sing your heart out to God."

She paused with her hand on the door, glancing back at him. "You really are serious, aren't you?"

"Didn't you tell me you had a Taylor guitar? Play it. We already know you have the voice of angel. Use it."

"If I can't sleep, I will."

"Something else. If Rabbi Cohen survives whatever happens tomorrow morning tell him I need to see him. I don't care if he thinks I'm a neo-Nazi or a reincarnation of Hitler or that I work for Hamas. Get him here. I have to show him something."

"Show him something? What do you have to show him except yourself?"

"Just make sure he comes to the jail."

Sierra winced and put her fingers to her forehead. "I have to lie down."

She pulled the door shut behind her and locked it.

Blackstone did not sleep.

He kept turning verses over and over in his head.

For though we walk in the flesh we do not war after the flesh, for our weapons are not carnal, but mighty through God to the pulling down of strongholds, casting down imaginations, and every high thing that exalts itself against the knowledge of God, and bringing into captivity every thought to the obedience of Christ, and having in a readiness to revenge all disobedience, when your obedience is fulfilled.

Guessing it must be close to dawn – he did not know the exact time for there were no windows and they had taken his watch – he spoke out loud from Isaiah 43.

But now thus says the LORD that created thee, O Jacob, and he that formed thee, O Israel, Fear not, for I have redeemed thee, I have called thee by thy name, thou art mine.

When thou pass through the waters, I will be with thee, and through the rivers, they shall not overflow thee, when thou walk through the fire, thou shalt not be burned, neither shall the flame kindle upon thee.

For I am the LORD thy God, the Holy One of Israel, thy Savior. I gave Egypt for thy ransom, Ethiopia and Seba for thee.

Since thou was precious in my sight, thou hast been honorable, and I have loved thee. Therefore will I give men for thee, and people for thy life.

He prayed it seven times.

Sweat glinted on his skin.

He was on his feet. He was on his knees. He prostrated himself before God. But not once did he lie on his back. Not once did he rest or drop off.

Behold, he that keeps Israel shall neither slumber nor sleep.

Yahweh is thy keeper, Yahweh is thy shade upon thy right hand.

The sun shall not smite thee by day, nor the moon by night.

Yahweh shall preserve thee from all evil, he shall preserve thy soul.

Yahweh shall preserve thy going out and thy coming in from this time forth, and even for evermore.

When he sensed the congregation had met somewhere for worship and that Sierra was singing before them he shouted three times, *Oh Israel, trust in the Lord, from this time forth for evermore! Oh Israel, trust in the Lord, from this time forth for evermore! Oh Israel, trust in the Lord, from this time forth for evermore!*

Then he was silent and stood facing the steel door that opened onto the cellblock.

An hour later it burst open, crashing against the cement wall.

The sheriff threw himself against the bars of Blackstone's cell, his face crimson and twisted. "The rabbi's own house. With his wife and kids. You're like another Timothy McVeigh."

Gibson and three other deputies were with him. He unlocked the cell and all four began to punch and kick Blackstone, cursing and yelling as they landed their blows. Blackstone dropped to the cement floor and covered his head with his hands, but the boots found his face and neck anyways.

"Stop it! Stop!" Sierra ran into the cell and had enough strength to peel two of the deputies off Blackstone and hurl them against the walls. "You know Rabbi Cohen and his family are fine!"

"Only because the rabbi had a sudden impulse to move everybody out of his house and into the park across the street." Sheriff Youngblood crouched so he could smack his fists into the top of Blackstone's head. "That gut instinct is the only reason fifty or sixty people weren't incinerated by a fire bomb."

Sierra gripped his arms. "No more!"

"Plenty more!" Youngblood knocked her back. "Subject attempted to escape custody, subject is dead!"

Rabbi Cohen, his black suit jacket a tangled mess, his black fedora absent, rushed into the corridor. "What's going on? What are you doing?"

Youngblood and Gibson were hauling Blackstone to his feet. Blood streamed over his cheeks and lips. The sheriff kneed him in the stomach.

"Just teaching him some manners, rabbi." Youngblood punched Blackstone in the head, knocked him down, and kicked him. "About what not to do on my watch."

Sierra sprang on Youngblood, growling, wrapping her arms around his throat, and squeezing as hard as she could. Pushing and shoving, Rabbi Cohen separated them, ramming the sheriff into one of his deputies while keeping a grip on Sierra.

"Has everyone in Diamondback gone crazy?" demanded Cohen. "Sheriffs acting like SS storm troopers? Perfectly normal girls violent and berserk? The fire bombings are hard enough to deal with. We don't need to tear one another apart as well." He released Sierra. "Get a cloth and water and clean Reverend Blackstone up."

"What are you doing here?" Youngblood shot Cohen a fierce look. "Shouldn't you be with your family and your flock? They've been traumatized. Your house and everything in it has been destroyed."

"And just like all the other fires you won't be able to tell me how it started or who did it. Except offer me your wild guesses." Cohen bent and helped Blackstone get up and sit on the cot. "Ms. Bloom said he wanted to see me and here I am. With my lawyer."

"Your lawyer?"

"That's right. Did you really think you could detain Pastor Blackstone indefinitely?"

"Of all people you want this arsonist back on the streets again, rabbi?"

"You had him locked in here and my house still blew up."

Youngblood thought a moment. "He has a team of conspirators. He sent them a message."

"How? By one of your deputies? No one knew I'd decided to hold the Sabbath service at my house until late this morning. We'd talked about renting the town hall. Why didn't they place an incendiary device there?"

"So what do you think? That it's something supernatural like Blackstone says?"

Cohen raised his eyebrows. "It was last time when all the pastors were being murdered."

"For pity's sake." Youngblood rolled his eyes up at the ceiling. "It was just a crazy minister and some MMA woman."

"That's not the way I remember it, sheriff. And you weren't here."

"Blackstone's trying to throw us off balance with all this hocus pocus."

"Nevertheless. We're walking Reverend Blackstone out of here."

"We just had a Nazi lawyer in here and Blackstone didn't want him. What makes you think he's changed his mind?"

"Is he a Jewish lawyer?" asked Blackstone as Sierra knelt and dabbed at the cuts on his face with a damp cloth.

"Is a rabbi going to offer you any other kind?" responded Cohen.

"I wish to speak with my client alone," announced a slender man with silver hair and sunglasses. He was standing just outside the cell in a white suit.

"The rabbi and Sierra can stay," Blackstone said, wincing as Sierra passed the cloth over the gouges at the side of his mouth.

"I'll leave a deputy behind," Youngblood grunted.

"You won't leave anyone behind we haven't consented to," the lawyer warned. "Or do I have to call in Federal marshals?"

"So you think you're going to just waltz him out of here, Mr. – ?"

"Victor Schultz. You don't have a shred of evidence against him. No proof that he's an arsonist. And then we have the interesting case of police assault against a prisoner."

"Suit yourself." The sheriff left the cellblock with his deputies. His eyes were slits when he glanced back at Sierra. "In case I forgot to tell you, Ms. Bloom, you're fired."

"Am I?" She did not turn to look at him, poking through Blackstone's hair for gashes. "I guess I must have anticipated you. I already put my note of resignation on your desk."

"Let's not jump too far too fast," Blackstone cautioned her.

"Actually I don't think any of us are moving fast enough," she replied, patting the cloth against the top of his head.

"Do you have a migraine?"

"No. But then I stayed up all night singing as you suggested. I'm only dead on my feet."

"I have a migraine," the lawyer complained, "and Tylenol with codeine won't touch it."

"I know how you feel, Victor." The rabbi massaged his forehead with his fingers. "Let's get out of here so I can go back to my family and my bed and lie down."

"Your house was set on fire?" asked Blackstone.

"Yes. It was a volcano. Just like Anaconda Vineyard and Beth Shalom. Everyone was well away from the blast.

I don't know why I decided to move everyone over to the park but I did. A minute later there was a bright flash and every part of the house was burning at the same time."

"Where are you staying?"

"With one of our families."

"Sierra's right. We aren't moving fast enough. John, I want you to rest up and then come over to my house tonight. I'm going to ask Father Eric from St. Michael's and Father Daniels from the Orthodox church in Missoula to join us. And Brett Sanders if he's up to it."

"What are we going to talk about?" asked Cohen. "Pain medication?"

"We're going to sing through the Psalms. What you call the Tehillim."

Cohen dropped his fingers, forgetting about his headache for a moment. "Jews and Christians singing the Tehillim together? Why?"

"We hold them in common. And they're the best antidote to what's caused the illness you and your lawyer friend Victor have picked up along with everyone else in Diamondback."

Victor removed his sunglasses. His eyes were gray and silver like his hair.

"And what exactly has caused my migraines, reverend?" he asked.

Blackstone closed his eyes as Sierra wiped dried blood off his eyebrows.

"Hocus pocus," he said.

4

Jude Aaron Blackstone's house
Saturday evening

"Most people will think they have gotten over the bug because their migraines have cleared up by now." Blackstone was leaning forward in the 1876 Morris chair in his living room. "All that means is they are fully infected and the virus has made a home in their mind and spirit. They will become more and more like the ones who put the curse, the supernatural bacteria, in the air to begin with. Sheriff Youngblood and his deputies were dead set against me this morning and last night. That will change rapidly. Soon they will be cheering me to the highest heavens because they think I have been depriving the Jews of their places of worship. They will begin to persecute the Jewish people in this community. So will thousands of others. You know the frenzy you have seen in the 1930s footage of Hitler's speeches? That is what will happen here over the next few weeks and months. Eventually there will be rallies and marches and Skeritt and his people will be at the center of them, swastikas waving. In time they will find excuses to kill men and women of the Jewish faith. And children. We will see pogroms. We will see Jewish homes and businesses vandalized and looted."

Blackstone glanced at Victor Schultz who leaned against the wall, arms folded, stoically maintaining an attitude of skepticism.

"Medical clinics and law offices will not be immune," Blackstone warned. "And law enforcement will look the other way or join in the attacks. People will be killed. Even children. Without regret or remorse. The Nazis call it the Dachau Blessing."

"How do you know all this?" The lawyer's face was as dark as a thunderhead. "You are making it up as you go. If others turn against us because of this, what will the Jewish people feel who are infected?"

"Some will feel self-loathing. Or they will be suicidal. Others will go along with whatever the authorities tell them to do. A good number will flee the county. A few will fight back. The Nazis wish the resistance aspect was not part of the spell but so far they haven't been able to do anything about it."

"The Dachau Blessing. What do you call it in your enlightened imagination, reverend?"

"I call it Treblinka Ghost. That's all. The spirit has been with us for a very long time. Since the beginning of time really."

"You believe in the devil?"

"The neo-Nazi leadership do and yes, Victor, I do as well. Believe me, many of the old Nazis of the 1920s and 30s and 40s had their share of occult beliefs and practices. Research it."

The skepticism remained on Schultz's face in lines that cut deeply into his skin. "Having such beliefs and having the power to do harm because of such beliefs are two entirely different things."

Rabbi Cohen began to recite, his eyes upon the wall and not making eye contact with anyone in the room.

How art thou fallen from Shomayim, O Heilel Ben Shachar, Bright One of the Dawn, Day Star, Lucifer! How art thou cast down to the earth, thou, which hast laid low the Goyim!

For thou hast said in thine lev, I will ascend into Shomayim, I will exalt my kisse above the kokhavim, above the stars of El. I will sit also upon the har mo'ed, the mount of assembly, on yarketei Tzafon, on the heights of Tzafon.

I will ascend above the heights of the clouds. I will make myself like Elyon, the Most High.

Yet thou shalt be brought down to Sheol, to the lowest depths of the bor, the pit.

"I speak from memory from Isaiah 14 in the Orthodox Jewish Bible," Cohen added. "My Christian friends would put it, *How art thou fallen from heaven, O Lucifer, son of the morning! How art thou cut down to the ground which did weaken the nations! For thou hast said in thine heart, I will ascend into heaven; I will exalt my throne above the stars of God. I will sit also upon the mount of the congregation, in the sides of the north. I will ascend above the heights of the clouds. I will be like the most High. Yet thou shall be brought down to hell, to the sides of the pit.*"

"That passage is about the king of Babylon," responded Schultz.

"You know Scripture can be understood on many levels, Victor," said Rabbi Cohen. "First and Second Enoch, books which our ancestors treated with great respect in the period of the Second Temple, considered these words from Isaiah to be referring to Satan. The Christians came to agree with that."

"It's time to worship." Blackstone picked up a guitar from its case by his feet. "Evil is fought in many ways.

Physically, which is why we must have the military and law enforcement, but also on a supernatural plane where guns and badges and law courts have no power. We are going to sing through all the Psalms or Tehillin. Some of the melodies you may know, some may be new. Regardless, I emphasize you must worship, not simply sing. This is not karaoke. True worship puts a heavenly shield around you, around all of us here tonight, and that shield will extend to the city and the county, everywhere the Nazi Satanist spell of evil has spread. They will most certainly know that the power of their enchantment is diminishing as we cry out to God and sing our praises to him. There will be retaliation that is both physical and supernatural. We must be prepared to counter both."

Sierra began to strum her Taylor and sing softly. *"Blessed is the man, the man who does not walk, in the counsel of the ungodly, blessed is that man. He who rejects the way, rejects the way of sin, and who turns away from scoffing, blessed is that man. But his delight, by day and night, is the law of God Almighty."*

Rabbi Cohen joined in. Then Father Eric of St. Michael's and the Greek Orthodox priest Father Daniel. Brett Sanders went to his knees as he sang, his eyes closed. Victor Schultz did not open his mouth in song until the second verse.

> *He is like a tree, a tree that flourishes,*
> *being planted by the water.*
> *Blessed is that man.*
> *He will bring forth fruit,*
> *his leaf will wither not,*
> *for in all he does he prospers.*
> *Blessed is that man.*
> *For his delight, by day and night,*

is the law of God Almighty.

Blackstone had never played guitar with Sierra before. There had never been the opportunity. She seemed oblivious to him, gazing into space as her left hand formed the chords, and he followed her lead, making every attempt to harmonize.

The ungodly are not so, for they are like the chaff,
which the wind blows clean away.
The ungodly are not so.
The ungodly will not stand upon the Judgment Day
nor belong to God's own people.
The ungodly will not stand.
But God knows the way of righteous man
and ungodly ways will perish.

As they moved through the Psalms, Father Eric sometimes broke into Latin, Father Daniel into Greek, his hands raised over his head, Rabbi Cohen worshipped in Hebrew, and Brett Sanders slipped back and forth between English and tongues, praising God in a heavenly language none of them could understand, but which all of them could feel exuded holiness. Every twenty-five Psalms they took a short break, Blackstone had laid out round loaves of fresh bread and spring water, then after ten minutes they would begin again. Some, like Brett Sanders and Rabbi Cohen, did not take any breaks at all, but remained in prayer, speaking to no one except God.

As the evening progressed, Blackstone remembered a gathering of worshippers in The Hague in the Netherlands, a few blocks from a high building called the *Hoftoren*. They had approval to hold a peaceful rally for two hours between ten and midnight and Christians from various churches gathered to light candles and sing hymns and worship songs. It was meant to be a night of prayer for the government of Holland, the international courts located in the city, and for the many embassies and EU institutions. Few knew what Blackstone knew, that Nazi Satanists were performing ritualistic ceremonies in a bunker far beneath the streets and avenues of The Hague. All the Nazis were doing would be blunted by the worship filling the physical and spiritual air of the Dutch capital. Blackstone expected the fascists to strike back against the churches and they did with fire bombings and an online campaign of threats and intimidation directed at pastors and their families. However this played into the hands of Blackstone's covert agency, *Dies Irae,* which battled criminal conspiracy and devil worship at an international level. Due to the physical assaults, they were able to bring in an elite Dutch counterterrorist unit, the UIM or *Unit Interventie Mariniers*, a Special Forces group comprised of marines from the *Korps Mariniers* or Netherlands Marine Corps. Storming the bunker in a top secret operation the public never heard about, returning rapid fire with their Heckler and Koch HK416 assault rifles, the UIM had put an end to Nazi Satanist activities in The Hague for years.

Joining in the assault on the Nazis, an HK416 in his grip, Blackstone had shouted one phrase in Dutch over and over again.

Laat je wapens vallen en geef je over!

Drop your guns and surrender!

As critical as the worship night was to combat the Nazi Satanists in Diamondback, Blackstone was well aware that if the Montana Justice Movement found their curses were blocked on a spiritual level, they would go on the offensive on a purely physical level, just as they had with the SS and the string of death camps like Treblinka and Auschwitz in World War Two.

The room seemed to be lit with fire when they finished singing at two in the morning, including Psalm 151 that was in the Orthodox Bible. One by one, as they drifted off into the warm August night, Blackstone said goodbye with a special blessing for each of them, even Victor Schultz, who still appeared reluctant to take the worship event and Blackstone's warnings seriously. Sierra lingered at the door.

"Listen," she said, "I never had a chance to apologize for the way I treated you at Anaconda Vineyard. I thought you'd lost it, screaming at us and shooting your pistol in the air."

"It's all right, Sierra."

"I clawed you and struck you and said terrible things. It's not all right."

"And I hit you like a football player."

"To save me. If you hadn't done that I'd have been killed when the church blew up."

"You didn't understand. And the spell was getting into your head. But you understand now, don't you?"

"Yes."

She reached out slowly for his face, unsure of how he might react to her touch. When he did not stop her hand or pull away, she placed her fingers gently against his skin.

"I have this crush on you," she said.

"Yeah?"

"For sure."

"So maybe you'll tell me your secret."

"What secret is that?"

"You have the coolest accent."

She smiled, the night and streetlights behind her, the guitar case in one hand. "And you want to know where it's from?"

"I think I know where it's from. I want to know how you got here."

"You are so smart you are going to answer your own questions? Where am I from, Mister Know It All?"

"The Netherlands. But which part I'm not sure."

She put one hand on her hip and cocked her head. "Guess."

"Zundert?"

"Zundert?" She stuck out her tongue. "No, not so. You thought because Van Gogh was born there this Little Dutchy might be born there too?"

"Well, both of you have to do with works of art. He made them and you are one."

"Ahhh." Her hand went back to his face and caressed it. "You and your words, hmm? Zundert is a beautiful place. So many fields, so many crops, so lush in the summertime. But I was born in Amsterdam. We moved to America when I was ten. My father works with Shell Oil. So my accent you think is so cool is an Amsterdam accent."

"Sierra. Beautiful Dutch woman. Be careful, okay? We talked about prayer and fasting so that we can keep blunting the Nazis' spells and curses. Our group's on a bit of a spiritual high right now and I'm not certain they picked up on my warnings about a very real physical threat in addition to the spiritual one."

"We did. But, honestly, what can we do if the sheriff is working against us?"

"He's going to flip-flop from one day to the next depending on which power has the ascendancy over him and his deputies. Some days he'll definitely feel it's in his best interests to back the Jewish and Christian communities. Other times he'll act like the most rabid anti-Semite and pro-Nazi. If things swing too far into the darkness we will see them joining the Montana Justice Movement and even taking part in their Satanism."

"That doesn't sound too promising, Jude."

"Some things are on our side. People outside of Diamondback, especially those outside our county, aren't tainted by the Satanic rituals. That's why Father Daniel could drive in from Missoula with a clear mind and a clear soul. Which means if they overdo the physical harassment we can call in law enforcement from outside Anaconda County and they won't be under Skeritt's control."

"Who's going to make that call? Youngblood won't."

"Maybe I can."

"*Maybe you can.* Some day you need to have a sit down with me and explain in great detail who you really are. But right now this girl needs to get home and get some sleep. I didn't get a wink last night, remember."

"I remember. Just be safe."

"God's watching over me, isn't he?" She was tall but still went up on her toes to plant a light kiss on Blackstone's lips. "And so are you, aren't you? What more does a girl from the Netherlands need?"

He watched her get into her Dodge Ram pickup and drive off in the dark.

Then he went inside to a small vault behind his fridge. In the vault there was an unregistered handgun, a SIG P227 with night sights and a fourteen round magazine that extended from the grip. It fired .45 ACP just like the UK USP that Youngblood had confiscated. A holster was also in the vault as well as a triple magazine pouch. Both would be concealed under the waistband of his jeans. He could not rely on the Sheriff's Office to protect him or anyone connected to the churches or the congregation of Beth Shalom. For that matter, he knew Native Americans, African Americans, Hispanics, and any citizens of Asian ancestry would not be safe in the weeks ahead. The neo-Nazis were about to unleash a race war.

He slept with his clothes on, fully armed. At Blue Sky Baptist's first Sunday service at eight o'clock there were about half the people he was used to, but at least those who attended seemed to be full of strength and faith. At ten, at the second service, the congregation was down by about two-thirds and bringing a message to them felt like trying to preach to a brick wall or Ezekiel's bed of briers and scorpions. He struggled, the worship team struggled, the strongest Christians he knew at Blue Sky Baptist appeared half-dead. The monthly potluck had about thirty people where there would normally be closer to a hundred and fifty or two hundred.

"Rodeo week's coming up," one of his elders said by way of explanation.

"Not for another five days," replied Blackstone.

The elder shrugged. "It's summer."

Blackstone had no intention of trying to get his leadership on track, not yet, not until things erupted on the streets that he could point to as requiring a season of extended prayer and intercession. He barely ate at the potluck and returned home to spend the rest of the afternoon and evening praying and sipping water purified by reverse osmosis, his choice when he could find it, buying Aquafina or Dasani. He also phoned The Seven as he had decided to nickname the group. Only Victor Schultz was not at home and he didn't return Blackstone's call. Not until the next day. Not until his law firm had its windows smashed, its carpets set on fire, huge swastikas painted in black on the walls of its offices, and TOD ZU

DEN JUDEN scrawled in blood on the furniture and ceilings.

Blackstone stood with Schultz and Rabbi Cohen and surveyed the damage.

"No one was killed?" asked Blackstone.

"I told you, no!" snapped Schultz.

"What about the blood?"

"They ran a test on that hours ago. It's pig's blood."

"Is that all the Sheriff's Office have done? Run pig's blood through the lab?"

"Pretty much. Youngblood wanted to know who we'd provoked to the point of outrage. Asked about our recent legal cases and if they'd all been above board. He acted as if the vandalism was our fault, that somehow we'd brought it on by unethical behavior."

"What else did he ask you?"

"How many Jews we had on staff."

Blackstone walked over the scorched carpets and examined each room. "It looks like photographs of *Kristallnacht, The Night of Broken Glass.* The pogroms the Nazis unleashed in Germany and Austria and the Sudetenland. Are you going to relocate?"

Schultz shrugged. "Two hours ago I thought Smith and Raymonds were going to let us rent the basement suites in their law office until our rooms were repaired. Fifteen minutes before you got here they phoned to call it off, said they needed the space now that we wouldn't be handling the caseload we normally would."

"Are they nabbing some of your clients?"

"Trying to."

"Did the press show up?"

"Not the locals. A CNN affiliate drove in and did sixty seconds of film. So did FOX."

"No notes left behind? No threats?"

"I think *death to the Jews* is pretty clear, reverend."

"It won't stop with this," Blackstone said to Cohen. "If they can get the support from the municipality they'll go after other businesses employing Jews."

"How can they get away with that? Helena will know. Washington will know."

"Just remember they have people in high places too."

"They can't have everyone in their pocket." Cohen had been holding his black fedora in his hand. Once they left the damaged building and were on the sidewalk, despite the warm late morning sun, he put it back on his head. "This sort of intimidation can't last long with the whole country watching. A phone call to the JDL, the Jewish Defense League, will change the picture pretty quickly."

"If the Nazis want to be subtle, they can be subtle, and still stick a knife between your ribs," Blackstone warned.

That week, one by one, members of Beth Shalom began to leave the synagogue. Some cited chronic illness. Some moved out of the county altogether. Some told Rabbi Cohen bluntly that their families had been threatened and that they would worship God in the privacy of their own homes from now on.

Others remained firm. They contacted the JDL but no representatives ever arrived in Diamondback. With Blackstone's help, Cohen appealed to Federal agencies that had offices in Diamondback. They were polite but unresponsive. Calls to Helena and Washington were put on hold or disconnected or never returned. Jewish members of Congress or the Senate did not get back to them.

"What is going on?" demanded Cohen. "The MJM and the neo-Nazis can't have that much power."

"That depends," replied Blackstone.

"On what?"

"On how much power you think Hell has."

"Doesn't Heaven have more?"

"Yes. But you have to want it."

"Of course I do."

"But not everyone does. Not among your people and not among mine."

Cohen closed his eyes as he stood beside Blackstone. "So then what do we do?"

"How many did Gideon have?"

"What?"

"How many men did Gideon have?"

"Why – " Cohen thought a moment. "He went from thirty-two thousand soldiers to ten thousand and finally to three hundred."

"Against how many?"

"And the Midianites and the Amalekites and all the children of the east lay along in the valley like grasshoppers for multitude; and their camels were without number, as the sand by the sea side for multitude."

"A handful facing a Blitzkrieg. Never mind the Spartans and their three hundred at Thermopylae. We are fighting for more than Sparta or Greece. And we are fighting for more than Israel or the Jewish people. It is a world we are trying to set free."

"So where are our three hundred?" asked Cohen.

"I will have to make some phone calls and send some emails," responded Blackstone. "Until then there is just the seven of us – you, me, Sierra, Victor Schultz, Father Eric, Father Daniel, and Pastor Brett Sanders. Our inner circle has seven. Skeritt's coven has thirteen."

"Phone calls? You're going to make phone calls? Haven't we already tried to do that?"

"I meant encrypted phone calls and encrypted emails."

Cohen stared at his friend. "You sound like the *Mossad*."

"Forget I even mentioned it."

"I have no idea what you're talking about."

Some days the Sheriff's Office swung to the side of Beth Shalom and the Jewish community and investigated ongoing incidents of vandalism and intimidation. Other days Youngblood and his deputies acted like the SS, threatening Rabbi Cohen and Jewish businesses themselves. When the annual rodeo parade of horses and marching bands and classic cars headed through the downtown on Saturday morning, the Montana Justice Movement and Lord of Lords church was in it, waving Nazi flags and chanting about God and white power, while Youngblood looked on with a smile of approval. Skeritt was dressed in a black SS uniform and rode a white stallion as thousands lined the streets cheering and applauding. That evening three young Hispanic men were beaten half to death at a bar a stone's throw from the parade route. Sunday night two shops owned and managed by Asian Americans were torched. An ABC film crew showed up but no one else. The Diamondback newspaper, The Rocky Mountain Record, wrote it up as a pair of shops with faulty wiring all installed by the same Jewish electrical company.

On Monday night Sierra called Blackstone in a panic.

"Jude, something's going on, there are people pulling up in front of my apartment."

"What sort of people?"

"I don't know any of them. But now Sheriff Youngblood is here in his patrol car."

"What's he doing?"

"Joining them. Jude, they – "

Sierra's cell went dead.

Blackstone was at her place in minutes.

Her door had been smashed open. Furniture overturned. A window shattered.

She was not there. No one was there.

A note had been placed on the fridge with a magnet that had a picture of a wolf.

On the note were two words in red marker.

BLOOD SACRIFICE

5

Tuesday night
24 hours later

One van was dark blue and battered. The other was white and battered.

Both had 2nd Amendment stickers on their rear bumpers.

Both sported Confederate flags from their aerials.

Both had gun racks in the cargo areas.

Both had Idaho plates.

Both were full of Israelis.

Both were parked in front of Jude Blackstone's house.

"Stay here," cautioned Blackstone. "Stay together. Your prayers are essential. They are the ultimate weapons."

The Seven sat together in Blackstone's living room. Without Sierra.

"Who's going to protect us if Sheriff Youngblood comes calling?" asked Victor Schultz. "I feel like I'm hiding in the Warsaw Ghetto."

"There are three soldiers from an elite Israeli counterterrorism unit on the grounds. Together they have more firepower than Youngblood and all his deputies. Or any SWAT team he may bring in for assistance. But don't worry. Soon enough he'll be responding to a 911 call from the Montana Justice Movement."

"What are you going to do? Start world War III?"

"Finish World War II."

"Exactly who are these Israeli soldiers?" demanded Schultz. "The Yamam? The Duvdevan?"

"Neither," said Blackstone. "You've never heard of their unit."

"And you know them how?"

"It doesn't matter."

"It matters to me. It's my neck. It's all our necks. How good are these guys?"

"It's Sierra's neck before it's yours or mine. I wouldn't trust her life to just anyone."

"For all we know she's already dead."

"Pray otherwise." Blackstone's eyes had gone a hard cold blue. "If she's dead I will tear this county apart to get every last one of her murderers."

"You are the weirdest Christian minister I've ever known. I wish I hadn't met you."

"*Di. Enough.*" Rabbi Cohen opened a Tanakh, a Hebrew Bible, which was on his lap. "From the Tehillim. Number 124. *If Adonai hadn't been for us — let Israel repeat it — If Adonai hadn't been for us when people rose to attack us, then, when their anger blazed against us, they would have swallowed us alive! Then the water would have engulfed us, the torrent would have swept over us. Yes, the raging water would have swept right over us. Blessed be Adonai who did not leave us to be a prey for their teeth! We escaped like a bird from the hunter's trap; the trap is broken, and we have escaped. Our help is in the name of Adonai, the maker of heaven and earth.*" He paused, his eyes moving from Father Eric to Brett Sanders to Father Daniel and finally coming to a stop on Victor Schultz. "Let us pray."

Blackstone changed into dark combat fatigues after he left the room.

When he slid in beside the driver of the blue van the man looked at him closely. "Our unit has trained together. We don't know you except by reputation."

"I'll work alone. You do what you do and I'll do what I do."

"I don't trust you. Why are we here? Why aren't SWAT or the Seals or Delta Force going in?"

"Because this is your job."

"*Lama?* Why is it our job?"

Blackstone brought a badge out of a pocket. It was a Star of David as black as the night sky. Except for a small line of silver Hebrew characters.

לעולם לא עוד

"How did you get that?" asked the driver in a harsh voice.

"I earned it. Braunau, Austria. 2009."

"You weren't there."

"*Betach.* Of course I was there. Didn't they brief you about me?"

"Sure, on the long military flight between Israel and the States. But none of it makes sense. I deal in real life. I don't send F16s to shoot down witches on broomsticks."

"Just neutralize the Nazis. I'll handle the broomsticks and black cats."

"Who you are and why the Americans aren't taking care of this is not clear in my head."

"You are *Le-olam Lo Od.* You are *Never Again.* You hunt neo-Nazis outside your borders. Just do it."

The driver started the engine and the headlights swept the darkness as the van moved ahead. The white van followed.

"Go two blocks and then take a left," instructed Blackstone.

"They will be waiting for us."

"We'll hide the vehicles a mile from the Montana Justice Movement compound. Yes, they'll be waiting for us. They wouldn't have told me they intended to use Sierra Bloom in a ritual sacrifice if they didn't want to draw me in and kill me."

"You believe in these Satanic rituals?"

"They believe in them."

"So maybe she is already dead."

"Turn right at the stop sign. Then go straight. You have maps of the compound?"

"Yes. And we spent two hours scouting out the place when we should have been sleeping."

"You know we have half an hour on their site? Tops? No engaging US law enforcement?"

The driver lifted one hand from the steering wheel. "Relax. It'll be okay."

"We lost three men in Austria."

"You were betrayed."

"That could happen here too."

"Not from my men."

"I am not thinking of your men."

The vans were driven into the trees and parked.

Then the eleven men began to make their way through the woods.

Blackstone led the way.

They had given him a TAR-21 or Tavor, a small but lethal bullpup assault rifle that he tucked tightly against the side of his body. It was named after the mountain where Barak and Deborah fought Sisera. It was also the mountain where Christians believed Jesus experienced the Transfiguration.

The driver had handed him a stainless steel 9mm pistol called a Jericho as well as the Tavor.

"I have a SIG," Blackstone argued. "It's a 45."

"What is your backup pistol?"

"The SIG's enough."

"Take the Jericho. A gift from the people of Israel."

"All eight million of them?"

"Sure. Their taxes paid for it."

Blackstone put it into a pocket on the hip of his combat jacket. *"Toda raba."*

"Bevakasha. This woman means a great deal to you?"

"I should have protected her. I should have been more careful. I knew how vicious these men could be. I was asleep on my feet."

"But you are not asleep now?"

"No."

"No." The driver had slapped him on the shoulder. "Rough them up."

Blackstone glanced at his watch. It was five minutes to three.

Now is the very witching hour of the night.

"Back at the vans no later than quarter to four," the driver whispered to Blackstone and the others. He said it again in Hebrew. "The password is *Oboz Zaglady.* Do not forget it. *Oboz Zaglady. Extermination Camp* in Polish. *B'seder?"*

Blackstone and the men nodded.

The driver looked at Blackstone. "I am Yoni. All right?"

"All right."

Yoni glanced at the others. "Mickey Marcus is on his own. But he will keep in touch with me. We want the woman alive. You have seen her photograph. We also want to put the Nazi leadership to bed. You have seen their photographs as well. Do not harm the Nazi women and their children. Be careful. These people expect Mickey to do something."

Despite the ice that was gathering force in his arteries and veins, Blackstone smiled. They had given him the name of the American officer who had fought with the Israelis during their War of Independence in 1948. Marcus had been appointed the first general or *Aluf* of the new Jewish nation.

"So we go. This is one of their weak spots."

Blackstone and the Israelis pulled black masks over their faces. There were holes for the eyes and mouth. Yoni slipped under a barbed wire fence and was gone. His men followed him into the dark of the compound.

Blackstone could not see any guards but he knew they were there.

He crouched and ran along the fence line.

One part of his mind was focused on getting into the compound close to the log church and finding Sierra. He was certain they would sacrifice her where their dark power and spirit of mockery would be greatest.

Another part of his mind was caught up in prayer.

Yet another replayed the events of the past twenty-four hours. He had used his secure cellphone for the first time since he had been transformed by plastic surgery and ended his covert work with *Dies Irae, Day of Wrath,* the ultra secret agency formed to combat devil worship and political intrigue at the highest levels of government worldwide. His request for assistance had been reluctantly granted and the black ops *Le Od* had been dispatched from Hatzor AFB near Gaza within an hour of his call. They had arrived at a military base in Anaconda County where it was understood they were to conduct joint exercises with US Special Forces in the mountains of Montana. Only two men knew the real reason the Israeli group was there and even they thought they were dealing with one of Israel's regular counter terrorist units.

The vans had been waiting in a motel parking lot in the closest town. Dressed in torn jeans and T-shirts the thirteen men had driven to Diamondback, recced the MJM property, and contacted Blackstone. He had given them maps Youngblood had drawn up after several visits to the compound when he had still been in a normal headspace. The Israelis had rented a couple of rooms at the Purple Sage Motel, grabbed four hours sleep, and parked at Blackstone's house in the dark. Three had hidden themselves among the bushes and trees in the yard.

Sierra had been kidnapped. But it was still a great risk to use a foreign black ops group to rescue her. Sheriff Youngblood could call in the FBI or Homeland Security. The Federal agents might not be under the spell when they arrived, but they could still get into a firefight with the Israelis, and that firefight could escalate into a crisis between Washington and Jerusalem. Clues were going to be left behind that made it look like a rival paramilitary group had raided the MJM compound for weapons and ammunition and explosives. But if Youngblood and his deputies showed up and were shot or killed things could get very nasty very quickly, especially if they called for backup from the Feds.

As your will is done in heaven may it be done on earth, my God. For others wish their will to be done. Wicked men with a wicked master who are opposed to your holy desires. Break them, Lord, break them and blind them, and may the pit they dig for others be the pit that devours them.

Yoni and the others were concerned about detection by guards and night vision devices. Blackstone was just as worried about being detected supernaturally. He knew the Nazis' inner circle of devil worshippers would be casting spells, probing the night, especially now that it was three o'clock, the hour they used to mock the Trinity, the hour that fell exactly half a day after the death of Christ on the Cross. They would try to bind and confuse Blackstone and whoever was with him. Failing that, they would resort to RPGs and assault rifles. His prayers and the prayers of the group meeting at his house were the highest form of spiritual resistance. Blackstone had even called upon God to release *the chariots and horsemen of Israel,* a prayer he only used under the worst circumstances.

And he answered, Fear not: for they that be with us are more than they that be with them. And Elisha prayed, and said, Lord, I pray thee, open his eyes, that he may see. And the Lord opened the eyes of the young man; and he saw, and, behold, the mountain was full of horses and chariots of fire round about Elisha. And when they came down to him, Elisha prayed unto the Lord, and said, Smite this people, I pray thee, with blindness. And he smote them with blindness according to the word of Elisha.

His earpiece came to life.
"It's a trap, Mickey!"
Gunfire erupted behind him in the compound.
Bright jagged flashes ripped open the dark.

A bomb burst in a shower of white sparks and flame.

Screams cut through his earpiece and then it went silent.

The light of the bomb showed at least a dozen men crouched around the church, assault rifles ready.

Youngblood and Gibson and two other deputies were among them.

One part of Blackstone froze.

How did they know? Why are they ready and waiting?

Another part went into action as soon as the glare from the blast faded away. He slid under the fence, got hooked by several barbs, ripped himself free, crawled to a hut he had seen in the bright stab of light, took a quart flask of gasoline from a pocket, sloshed some around the base of the hut which he could see was an outhouse, made a trail as he backed off into a cluster of bushes, and used his Zippo. There was a loud *whoosh* as the gas ignited and flames speared the dark. The men surrounding the church opened up immediately, calling out to each other and spraying the night with bullets. Blackstone kept his head down. As the hut flared up and began to burn fiercely he took out his SIG 227, used the night sights to line up a man with a shaven head, fired twice, rolled, got up on his elbows, held his breath, aimed at another skinhead, did another double tap, and rolled again, hugging the ground in a thick patch of darkness. The response by way of automatic fire was heavy and prolonged.

You chose correctly, Blackstone. We are in the church and preparing Sierra for the sacrifice. An expert practitioner will drain the blood perfectly into the bowl and then hurl the contents of the bowl into the magic fire. You will not be able to withstand the power we unleash with this blood ritual; I don't care how fervently you believe or how hard you pray. We call upon the Dark

Spirit of the Apocalypse, we call upon The Horsemen, and the White Christ But you could call upon the White Christ too. You could worship him and his offspring that live among us. It's not too late, reverend.

It was Skeritt's voice in his head.

Blackstone knew he only had minutes.

They would not lose the opportunity of the Witching Hour to take Sierra's blood.

He prayed in a low voice as guns crashed around him.

He knew Skeritt would hear him.

"My father, my father, the chariots and horsemen of Israel!"

Within seconds, Yoni's voice filled his earpiece.

"Avi, Avi! The merkavah of Yisroel and the parash thereof!"

Blue fire exploded all around the church as half a dozen Tavors erupted. The Nazis staggered and tumbled. So did Youngblood and his deputies. Blackstone sprang to his feet, sprinted to the church, threw himself into a window, rolled on the floor as glass shattered over his head and bullets zipped by his body, jumped into a crouch, acquired his black-robed targets immediately with his Tavor, and began to fire rapidly, sweeping the front of the sanctuary and avoiding the altar where Sierra was robed, on her back, and probably drugged.

For a moment Blackstone saw a curl of black light intertwining with a snake-like spiral of red. It was swelling to life in the air over the altar. A skull formed, a long-handled scythe, a horse's head, teeth, ragged manes that seemed mixed with blood and fire, a roar of hooves filled the church, a shriek of screaming mares and stallions. Then Skeritt, who had been facing Blackstone defiantly with his arms outstretched, calling out to Satan in Latin, was cut in half by the Tavor's bullets, and with a look of shock and

82

rage, the upper half of his body sagged to the right, and the bottom half fell to the left. Enough blood and oxygen remained in Skeritt's brain for him to recognize Blackstone when Blackstone took the mask from his face and stood over the Nazi leader.

"They overcame him by the blood of the Lamb, the word of their testimony, and because they did not love their lives so much they were afraid to face death," Blackstone said. "You have seconds to say yes to the Lamb, Skeritt, seconds to say yes to the Lion. The true Christ who did really die on the Cross and not take a boat to Magna Germania. Or it is the Great Darkness."

Skeritt's blue eyes tried to focus on Blackstone.

But the light left them as if someone had clicked a switch.

Blackstone scooped Sierra up from the altar.

Her blue eyes had the color and illumination Skeritt's had lost.

But they could not find Blackstone.

"It's the drugs." Yoni was at his side. "Bring her. The sheriff called for help when the shooting started. I have his cellphone. We saw the number to the FBI office in Missoula. They will send choppers."

"What other numbers did you see?"

"They mean nothing to me. But I have the cellphone in my pocket." He began to run from the church, Tavor ready. "*Yella, yella!* Let's go!"

Blackstone sprinted after him with Sierra in his arms, holding her face close to his. "Is the sheriff dead?"

"No. But his deputies are."

"Are we going back to the vans?"

"There isn't enough time. Someone let these people know we were coming. We have to assume the Nazis and Youngblood knew everything about us. So the sheriff may have told the FBI about the vans, even given them descriptions and license plates. We are taking two of the MJM's Broncos. By the time the FBI arrive, and the Nazis tell them about the stolen vehicles, we will have exchanged them for two others in Diamondback and be well on our way to the military base."

Two bodies were laid out in the back of the Bronco that Blackstone climbed into.

"What happened?" he asked Yoni.

"When we were ambushed. At the beginning. A grenade killed Uri, machine gun fire took Yitzhak."

"I'm sorry."

"We killed the skinheads that trapped us. My men are avenged."

As Blackstone cradled Sierra's head, the two Broncos roared out of the compound. No one fired or attempted to stop them. The headlights showed bodies to the left and the right. Blackstone spotted a white flag with a black swastika draped from a tree. The numbers 88 and 14 were at two corners of the flag, a wolf's head and Odin's Cross at the others.

"What's that flag?" he asked Yoni.

"The Colorado Saxons. A white power group. It's only been in existence six months."

"I haven't kept up on my neo-Nazi homework. What about the numbers?"

"The 88 is for Heil Hitler – H is the eighth letter of the English alphabet. The 14 is for a sentence an American neo-Nazi wrote in prison that a number of right wing groups have adopted. It is honored the way evangelical Christian honor John 3:16 or an Orthodox Jew venerates the Tetragrammaton. *We must secure the existence of our people and a future for white children.* Indications the attack was carried out by The Colorado Saxons are littered over the compound. We even shouted that to skinheads during the firefight. *You are too soft on the Jews and the blacks! You play footsies with the Indians! You must be like the Saxons! We will put white blood back into you! We will put steel!"*

"May I see the sheriff's cellphone?"

Yoni tossed it to him.

Blackstone checked the call log. He could see that Victor Schultz had phoned Youngblood more than a dozen times. The most recent had been two hours before. He slipped the phone into a pocket.

"Anything?" asked Yoni.

"Something."

"You must tell me. Two of my men are dead."

"I will introduce you." He kissed Sierra's hair and cheek as they sped along the highway, then placed his lips on the pale curve of her own. "You were complaining of a headache earlier, Yoni. How is that?"

"It's gone. The fighting cleared my head." He glanced at Blackstone. "You did well for a *goy.*"

"Such a compliment."

"She will be all right."

"I hope so. I don't know what they used."

"My father and my grandfather are both rabbis. Trust me, I feel her spirit, she will be all right." He smiled. *"L'shana habaah b'yerushalayim. Next year in Jerusalem."*

"L'shana habaah b'yerushalayim. Next year in Jerusalem."

EPILOGUE

"So now we are supposed to go back to life as normal?"

"As much as we can, yes."

"How can I work for the sheriff again?"

"Because you know he was under a spell."

"He scarcely remembers it."

"Not so bad a thing."

"Bad if it happens all over again." Sierra tugged Blackstone down into the tall green grass on the riverbank. "Are you going to tell me what happened to Victor? I hate loose ends."

"There are always loose ends. He left with the special ops team that liberated you. That's all we know."

"Three weeks have gone by and not a word from him."

Blackstone shrugged. "He'll show up eventually."

"And who were the people who rescued me?"

"Can't say."

"Can't say or won't say?"

He shrugged again.

"And where have the white supremacists gone?"

"Oh, maybe to start a war in Colorado."

"What? You mean with that group FOX says raided the compound? The Saxons? Which makes no sense in terms of a hostage rescue. They certainly didn't back you up, did they?"

"I'm kidding. You know the FBI found enough evidence of criminal activity to arrest the MJM leaders who survived the raid, right? The rest of them have moved on. Maybe back to Idaho. The property's up for sale. Want to move in?"

"With you?" Sierra laid her head in his lap and her blue eyes took in the sun that was just about on top of them. "We haven't even kissed yet."

"I did. When you were in my arms. After the rescue."

"What?" She almost sat up.

"It wasn't a very long kiss. You were cold and frozen. Like some sort of beautiful statue. I thought if I could kiss you, like a fairy tale prince, you would be all right."

"And turn into what exactly? You tell me all the time how stunning I am. Where does a girl go from there?"

Blackstone's hand moved along the side of her face and stroked back her fine blonde hair. "You go to a place beyond words. A place where you take my breath away and steal my mind so that I have nothing to say, nothing to think, all I can do is love you and hold you like fire holds a burning forest."

"You and your lines! You drive me crazy, American boy!" Her hand went behind his head and brought his face down to hers. "Wait. Did you just say you loved me?"

"I almost lost you. Going into that compound that's what drove me. Loving you and loving God."

"It turned out to be a potent combination." Her lips hovered by his but did not touch. "Someone stuck a note in the pocket of that awful robe the Satanists had me in. When I came out of the drug haze and changed I found it."

"I didn't do it."

"I know you didn't do it. But it was about you. They wrote that you ran through a firestorm of bullets to save me. Is that true?"

"It didn't say that."

"It did say that."

"There were a lot of bullets flying around for sure. I couldn't let something as minor as that stop me."

"Funny boy."

"You know, I'm not supposed to fall in love. I'm not supposed to get emotionally involved with a woman."

"What are you talking about?"

"But that was another life and it was a very long time ago."

"Good." Both Sierra's hands interlaced at the back of Blackstone's head. "Because no one's ever saved me before. So do you mind if we kiss all day and all night? By way of celebrating that very dragon and castle and hero and damsel event that was my salvation? Do you mind if we kiss until we forget all the evil in the world and remember only the good?"

"It's worth a try."

"Yes, it is." She brought his mouth even closer. "Let's experiment."

She brought their lips together and Blackstone took in all her heat and sweetness and strength in a rush. And it worked. Nazis and their swastikas were gone from his head. Devil worshippers and their incantations. Evil men with evil designs and evil followers. A world of dark against light, a world of heaven against hell. It was all gone as her kisses burned and intensified and worked their way right down into the deepest part of his soul.

But in the morning the sun rose again and a broken world with it.